Still Waters

Five Stories
By Thom Brucie

Introduction By
Ron Hugar

FIRST EDITION - TIGHT CURTAIN PRESS
SECOND EDITION - DANIEL'S VISION PRESS
e-book - MILSPEAKBOOKS

Printed in the United States of America
and committed to the standards set by
the Green Press Initiative

Daniel's Vision Press
J. Michael Bibb, Editor

ISBN: 978-0-9887094-0-9

Grateful acknowledgment is made to the following journals in which some of these stories first appeared:

"Maybe a Lesser Sin"
in *Schuylkill*
"Benjamin Uriah and the Golden Gate Bridge"
in *Pacific Review*
"A Deepening Heart"
in *Battle Runes: Writings on War*

For Theresa, Jason,
Derrick, and Heather

Contents

Introduction

Ron Hugar

Since the beginning of his professional training as a writer, Thom Brucie has maintained that the hallmark of a true writer of fiction is the ability to tell a story. The following collection, *Still Waters*, is a testament to his unswervable belief that a piece of fiction must be a successful story first, regardless of what other qualities the work may display.

Nearly anyone can tell a story, and, in fact, we tell a story to nearly everyone we meet in the course of a day. Whether or not the stories are engaging depends upon a number of factors within and without the control of the storyteller. I see three factors as crucial in constructing an engaging story:

1. choice of details, facts and incidents;

2. the communication of human experience as narrative purpose;

3. the use of voice, language, and voice as language.

Most obviously, stories are always teleological in their construction. Each and every detail, fact, and incident must be relevant to the end of the story, or, more accurately, to the end purpose of the story. Storytellers walk a fine line here: Too many facts, details, etc., and the purpose of the story may come across as heavy handed; too few, and the purpose may be lost in a fog of audience confusion, inattention or misapprehension.

The ability to choose facts, details and incidents appropriately, as well as the skill to weave them together in a way that the reader willingly comes along for the ride, depend on the storyteller's understanding of his audience and the world the audience navigates every day. However, a good storyteller understands that taking the quotidian experience of every audience member and engagingly communicating a purpose requires the ability to present that shared, quotidian experience in a way that shifts the perspective of the human experience of the everyday to a perspective of everyday experience as an experience of the unusual, if not the eternal.

This, of course, requires that the storyteller and the audience share a set of values and cultural experiences that allows for a kind of intellectual shortcut to the chase. However, for a storyteller to tell a story engagingly he must bring his reader to those shortcuts from a road less traveled, through uncharted forests, so to speak. At the beginning, the destination should be shrouded in mystery, but, at some point in the tale, the audience should catch a subliminal glimpse of the destination and marvel at the route chosen.

The story, "Memory Basket," illustrates this principle perfectly. A single mother with a dying daughter has all the potential of a melodramatic tearjerker – what once would have been second tier, "B" movie material. However, Brucie manages to change that. As he builds the relationship between mother and child, he also builds the generational relationship between grandmother and granddaughter. In the end, the grandmother's presence in the lives of the living is otherworldly without being ghostly. In other words, "Memory Basket" illustrates the truth that memories transcend not only time and death but also they provide mortal humans a path to a justice and peace separate from the life and death truth of our lives.

We find the same strategy employed in a slightly different way in "Maybe A Lesser Sin." This story seems to emanate from an earlier generation. A first-generation American venerates his immigrant grandparent whose patriarchal authority is old-world and at odds with the new-world organization of the family. However, soon we begin to understand that "Maybe A Lesser Sin" is a story about the spiritual relationships between men who live in the world and men who live of the world – and, how an authoritarian church mediates the lives of the two. The old-world/new-world dichotomy of earlier tales provides the loose framework of Brucie's story, but in the end, the old-world/new-world dichotomy is erased by the conflict between church power, temporal power, spiritual truth and the tragedy of the conflict between familial responsibility, religious responsibility and misdirected love.

American society places great emphasis on the uniqueness of the individual, and much has been made of the idea of "voice" within fiction. "Voice" is thought to be an ineffable quality, a mix of attitude, language use and perspective that is unique to a particular writer/storyteller and which functions as a kind of "signature" that renders a story as undeniably the work of that particular author. The pith of the metaphor works because in our daily lives we often identify persons close to us by the timbre, pitch and cadence of their voices, which is how we can recognize who is at the other end of a telephone line without them identifying themselves. However, the idea of "voice" as it is too often used in much criticism and theory implies that artistic affect is dependent on "voice." This attitude, however, works to obscure the interaction of character, setting and plot which are the real building blocks of both story and affect. The personality of an effective storyteller never intrudes into the story, just as the personality of an effective stage actor never alters the narrative truth of the character portrayed. All this is not to say that "voice" is not a legitimate conceptual tool of criticism. The distinction is one between performer and storyteller. A performer performs a story, and the pleasure and interest for the audience reside mainly in the performer's performance of it. On the other hand, the "voice" of a read story (as opposed to a performed one) should reside in the personality of the narrator.

The voice of the first person narrator provides the audience the perspective necessary to discern the narrative purpose of the story. American regionalist writers such as Bret Harte and, to a certain extent, Mark Twain, construct character, plot and purpose through the use of a narrator whose language is tied to the geographical region in which the action unfolds. Word choices, dialect, and cadence provide the audience clues to the perspective the storyteller wants the audience to take on the purpose of the story. These qualities of voice also map out the terrain of the route to be taken, generally to both familiarize and to gently alter the audience's access to their interpretative experience. Finally, the language of the everyday is altered in such a way that a shift in social perspective for the audience becomes possible.

In Harte and Twain's time, dialect also served as an introduction to the social and cultural differences that characterized the many different regions of the newly developing United States. Whereas today, dialect is often seen as caricature and, therefore, demeaning. In "Benjamin Uriah and the Golden Gate Bridge," Brucie uses the dialect of the first person narrative as a device to set the historical period and social standing of the narrator. The dialect of the narrator gives the audience a foothold for accessing the period and working-class milieu crucial to the humor of the tale.

The first person narrator of "The Executor" is more contemporary in his language use, though dialect is still evident. Here, the language used serves to emphasize the nature of the long-term relationship between the narrator and the two main characters of the story. When the narrator says, "Robbie got this pansy job baby-sitting a bunch of ROTC cadets," the audience immediately knows the tenor of the relationship between these long time friends. The hint of a testosterone-driven relationship found in the phrasing sets up the circumstance which drives the irony that closes the narrative and provides dimension to the narrative purpose of the story.

The influence of the voice of an omniscient narrator on the narrative purpose of a story is more difficult to discern. Postmodern theory acknowledges that cultural and social perspectives are always at work in language, and, as such, influence both the audience's understanding of a story and a storyteller's construction of that story. Modernist theories of language insist that meaning in language is transparent. Thus, an omniscient narrator has little to no effect on the narrative purpose of a story. In effect, according to modernist narrative theory, the purpose of the story was preordained and the omniscient narrator merely relays the facts of the matter.

Regardless of which theoretical perspective an audience chooses to explain the relationship of an omniscient narrator to meaning in language, an omniscient narrator for a storyteller has but one main duty: to develop narrative purpose. "A Deepening Heart" strikes me as an exemplary model of how an omniscient narrator should function within a story. To a certain extent, the storyteller uses the omniscient narrator to allow the audience to eavesdrop on the thoughts of the protagonist. Since the narrative purpose of many of Brucie's stories depends upon spiritual value as human motivation, glimpses into the mental lives of his protagonists are essential to understanding his narrative purposes. In essence, the voice of Brucie's omniscient narrators provide the audience with the language needed to access and understand his narrative purpose. The omniscient narrators of both "A Deepening Heart" and "Memory Basket" provide that access in a completely unobtrusive manner. The narrator of "Maybe A Lesser Sin," on the other hand, provides access to the thoughts and motivations of the main character, Alisio, through interjection that borders on first person. However, Brucie avoids a first person bias in "Maybe A Lesser Sin" by presenting Alisio's thoughts via verse. By presenting the first person experience of Papa Drapo via dialogue, Brucie uses an omniscient narrator to contrast the nature of the loves motivating the two main characters.

The dominant theme of the stories in Still Waters is that of human endurance within the truth of eternal justice founded in love. Without exception, each story depends upon the truth of love in the human experience and how human surrender to that truth brings peace and justice to each of the protagonists. For this reason alone, the stories contained in this collection are well worth the time and effort to read and contemplate. They are a testament to Thom Brucie's skill as a storyteller and faith in the truth of love within the human spirit.

Ron Hugar
August, 2006

The Lord is my shepherd,
I shall not want.
He makes me to lie down in green pastures;
He leads me beside the still waters.

(Psalm 23:1-2)

Maybe a Lesser Sin
_____

Idid not want to watch my grandfather die
       but I did
as surely as I watched him
prune his grape vines
as truly as I watched him
eat sweet meat
rolled in oregano
bathed in olive oil
fried in re-used fat.

Papa Giovanni Drapo was the head of the family, the strongest. He ruled with unquestioned authority. He brought his family from Italy to the hills of northern Pennsylvania after World War I to be free and to work the railroads. He loved the beauty of the rolling hills, especially in fall when maple leaves prospered like fireworks and the evening winds carried the early nibble of winter. With the pruning of his grapevines in November of 1959, Papa Giovanni Drapo turned eighty-three. He also began to die.

What do the saintly old ones know of death
with the hair growing out of their ears
and their eyes set deep
at the back of their noses
squinting even when the sun is behind
dull clouds?
Why am I threatened by hair
when there are so many other dangers
like secrets which only appear
when I am not ready for them?

He was dying, but no one cared. The members of his family regarded Giovanni's rule with disdain. Only Alisio interpreted Giovanni's dictatorship as the strength which bound the family together. So no one cared that Giovanni was dying; no one except Alisio. Alisio loved his grandfather, but he never told him, because Papa Giovanni's men did not speak of love. Men were men. Men were strong.

Alisio was twenty-seven. Since his return from World War II, he went to Mass every morning, for he believed it was God who preserved him from death in the war. He had black hair and Papa's great brown eyes set deep near the bone of his nose. Every day he tried to get old Giovanni back to church.

"Come to church, Pa," Alisio pleaded. "Have confession. Take communion."

"No, Alisio," Papa said. "No church. Since Father Anselmo condemned me and my sin, I don't go to church never again."

Papa didn't go to church. Alisio did, and he

prayed for Papa.

Now Papa lay in bed, the crucifix above his head, and Alisio, knowing death, hung a rosary on the bedpost. This day Giovanni Drapo was not strong. He was weak. The huge brown eyes looked heavy as pewter and dull as a pruned vine cracked by frost. Alisio knew from war that distant look in the eye. Dead eyes look away from this world.

Alisio had watched other men die, but he did not want to watch his grandfather die. He took one hand and held it, clasped it in his own. The hand was long, bony now, without power.

Tiny white whisker stubs roughened Giovanni's face. Large white hairs curled from the soft lobes of his ears. His cheeks were sunken and gaunt, but he still had all of his teeth. Papa never brushed his teeth; he wiped them clean with a towel after he ate.

"Pa," Alisio said, "you're eighty-three years old. You're weak. Let me call the priest."

Papa rolled his head quietly toward Alisio. He smiled.

"I was a strong man," Papa said.

"Yes, Pa."

"You know about the wheel, Alisio?"

"Yes, Pa." He knew.

***

Giovanni Drapo was the strongest man who ever worked for the railroad, strong as the coal of his beloved mountains. Many crews of Italian immigrants worked the rails during the depression. Giovanni,

Giuseppe, Tommaso, and Roberto were a crew. Giovanni was crew leader. Their job was to replace the great wheels of the boxcars. Each steel wheel weighed six hundred and thirty-seven pounds. To set the wheel, the crew raised one corner of the car above level with a hand jack.

"Raise 'em up a little bit more," Giovanni would order Tommaso.

Standing back, his practiced eye would judge just the right height.

"That's good," Giovanni would yell and pronounce the height correct by crossing his hands and arms like an umpire shouting `safe.'

Roberto greased the axle. Giuseppe set the guide pin. All four men circled the iron wheel. Giovanni shouted, "Now!" and together they lifted. They shifted the weight abruptly. Giovanni always took the lower grasp, the heaviest downthrust. Then, in harmony, they slid the wheel onto the axle.

"Hey, Giovanni," Tommaso teased, "why do you always take the bottom? Why don't you switch around?"

"Whatta you, stupid? You wanna kill somebody?" Giovanni answered. "What if the wheel falls?"

"What, you never gonna drop the wheel? Maybe we better change before you drop one and it kills somebody."

"I don't drop the wheel. How many times I gotta tell you? I'm stronger than all three of you bums."

That day Tommaso was in a playful mood, and

4

he changed the banter of their game.

"Hey, Giovanni," he smiled, "why don't you prove to us how strong you are? Why don't you set a wheel by yourself? What do you think, Giovanni, you really stronger than three men?"

He gazed at his crew. They stopped drinking their wine. They each returned his stare.

"I don't do your work for free," he coaxed. "You put up some money, I set your wheel. What kind of bet you gonna make?"

The crew averaged three wheel settings per day. Each man received as pay three dollars, American, per day. The challengers hesitated.

"Okay," Giovanni said, "I'll make it easy for you. Three dollars. That's what I bet. Three dollars."

Giuseppe, Tommaso, and Roberto eyed each other, a gleeful anticipation jumping at their cheeks.

"A dollar each will buy lots of bread," Tommaso said to the others. "One man cannot pick up a wheel and set it. Why don't we take this bet? I can use the money. Besides, maybe we'll humble Papa a little so he don't brag so much at lunch, and we can digest our food."

The others laughed.

"Okay, Giovanni," they agreed. "Three dollars."

"What are you gonna tell Mama when you miss a whole day's pay?" Tommaso teased.

The three sat back. Waited.

Giovanni continued to stare at them. Without moving, he said, "No."

"What do you mean, `No'?"

"No," he scowled.

"Hey, you made the bet, Giovanni. What's the matter? You chicken?"

"No," Giovanni repeated. He pointed an iron finger at them. "Three dollars each one of you."

The men stopped laughing.

"Each one of us?" Tommaso asked.

"Three dollars, each one," Giovanni repeated.

"Giovanni," Roberto said, "you make fun. Nobody can lift a wheel by himself. Nobody can bet a whole day's pay."

"Three dollars. Each one. I pick the wheel. I set it. All by myself. I'm stronger than you three put together, but you gonna pay to see."

Giovanni stood. His chest breathing deeply. His sharp eyes bright.

The crew looked with raised eyebrows to one another.

"No one man can possibly set one of our wheels," Roberto repeated. "But a whole day's pay." He shook his head. "Papa Giovanni is strong, but . . ."

"No," shouted Tommaso. "No man is as strong as you claim. I will bet three dollars."

Encouraged by this, the others agreed.

Giovanni made careful preparation. He set the jack tight under the collar. He applied grease to the wheel hole and to the axle. He set the guide pin at precisely thirty degrees. He took his time. Only with correct preparation could a wheel be set.

The others grew bold and confident. They drank more wine.

Giovanni cleared the path he would take,

adjusted the guide pin one slight fraction, and sucked a powerful, deep breath.

Cautiously, he straddled the wheel. His massive fingers spread around the edges, gently, deftly, testing the balance, lifting slightly, re-adjusting. His shoulders convexed, and his thighs riveted, and the veins at his neck inflated, and Giovanni raised the six hundred and thirty-seven pound wheel to ankle height. He shuffled his cargo toward the box car, and in one extraordinary lift raised the wheel above the axle, tilted it slightly with his left hand to catch the guide pin and, flicking his wrists simultaneously, slid the wheel into place.

Sweat ran from the pores on his face and arms. His chest raised and lowered like a piston. He shut his eyes, raised his arms above his head, clenched his hands into fists and exhaled like a bellow of locomotive steam. He won. He always won.

**

"Yes, Pa," Alisio repeated. "I know about the wheel. You were a strong man."

Everyone knows about the wheel, Pa, Alisio thought. You made sure everyone remembered. When Tommaso refused to pay, you broke his finger. The next day when he did hand you the money, you made him work an extra shift. The men said you were out of line, but I understood that Tommaso earned his money back on the extra shift.   Why could they not see him as Alisio did? Papa was no saint. He shouted at everyone. He chased the children with his cane. He was unapproachable. But, Alisio also knew, he kept the family together through the trauma of immigration, through the devastation of the depression, and he kept them together now. How many men are there whose family spans four generations?

Alisio looked at this grandfather who had ruled so strongly, so without question. He probed the weakened arms and traced the shallow, withered chest with his eyes. He's a good man, a caring man, Alisio thought. He just didn't know how to tell anyone.

Alisio spoke his thoughts. "You were a strong man, Pa. And a good man."

"No, Alisio," Giovanni clutched at him. "I'm not a good man. Father Anselmo said no man is forgiven for what I did."

"Papa," Alisio urged again. "Please let me call the priest."

But Papa did not listen. These past few years he would go out of contact more and more. He'd fade away mentally. Then he'd babble.

"Stop. Stop," he'd yell. "No. No," he'd scream. "Come back, my baby," he'd call. His arms reached to some unknown someone. His eyes talked to some unseen ghost. Papa's breathing rattled a little, but even in his delusion he clung to Alisio with silent, bony fingers, and Alisio knew he would not watch Papa die much longer.

***

"Alisio. Alisio. Quickly. You've got to do something."

8

"What is it, Aunt Rosa?"

"It's Papa. He's talking to himself. He won't let little Tony up from the table. I'm afraid, Alisio. Do something."

Alisio walked to the kitchen. It smelled sweet, like warm sauce. Papa sat at the front of the wooden table. Three quarters of the wine bottle was empty. Papa cleaned his teeth with a white dishtowel.

"Tony, eat your food," Papa spoke to the boy.

Tony's plate was clean except for some bread crust. He wanted to go play, but he knew Papa's discipline could be painful. So he sat.

"Goddammit, Tony," Papa shouted, "eat your food."

Alisio walked around the table and stood behind Tony.

"Papa," he said, "Tony's done eating. He wants to play now. Pour me some vino, and we'll talk."

Alisio touched Tony's shoulders. The boy rose and walked toward the back door.

Without warning, Papa grabbed a fork and flung it at the boy. The fork spun, end over end, just past Tony's ear, and the tines pierced the door casing.

"Goddammit, Tony, eat your food. You leave when I tell you."

No one moved.

Then Papa Giovanni seized a glass, filled it with wine for Alisio, and motioned Tony out to play with the flick of his hand.

Alisio was patient. He knew this insanity was

9

temporary and would pass. Papa was getting old.

> Oh, dementia,
> flower of forgetfulness
> thy fragrance puts to sleep
> the inconsequential
> the foolish the unnecessary,
> and soft tulip of ripe lunacy
> thy attraction is to sanity
> as color to the bee.
> Oh, sparkling blue and yellow
> and red dots of blinking dementia,
> thy hypnosis is less understood
> than thy behavior
> for whosoever seeks thee
> he shall find,
> and whosoever finds thee
> he is lost.
> Oh, sweet dementia,
> how stained is thy sparkling attraction
> how dark thy brilliant trap.

The crisis passed with no one hurt, but the family grew fearful.

"What if he tries to do something with his shotgun?" Aunt Rosa asked. "He's so strong, who would stop him if he went into a rage?"

Papa's shotgun was the only earthly possession in which he held pride. In Italy, he had fought the mafiosi. The trusted 12 gauge had saved his life, and he prized it above all things.

"You've got to get the gun from him, Alisio,"

pleaded Aunt Rosa. "Tell him you're going hunting or something."

"I've never lied to him, Aunt Rosa. I can't start now."

"Tell him anything, but get the gun. You're the only one he'll listen to."

When they were alone, Alisio said, "Pa, let me have your gun."

Papa Giovanni gave him the gun without comment.

Four months later, Alisio walked past Papa's house on the way home from work.

"Alisio," Papa called.

"Hello, Pa."

"Alisio, come here."

Alisio walked to the porch. Papa rocked gently, pushed off the floor with his toes. His cane lay across the arms of the chair. Papa looked straight ahead while he rocked.

"You got my gun?" asked Papa.

"Yes."

"You bring it to me," he ordered.

"You want the gun, Pa?"

"Yes. You bring it now."

Alisio walked home and returned with Papa Giovanni's 12 gauge. He stepped to the porch and handed him the weapon.

Papa cocked the barrels open. He checked for rust; felt for oil. He snapped it shut. Papa Giovanni slapped his hands smartly around the shotgun and held it in front of him, elbows locked.

He looked at Alisio.

"Now," he said, "the gun is yours."

***

Oh, Papa, Alisio thought, you're going to die outside the Church, and there's nothing I can do, and I haven't even shaved you today.

"You're a good boy, Alisio. Stay with your Papa."

"You need a shave."

"No. No time," he said.

Papa seemed exceedingly tiny. He was dwarfed by the greatness of the pillow at his head and by the thickness of the blanket.

Death must, like silver echoes,
roll gently against the back
of a fortress mountain we call
tomorrow,
a time far off
and distant, like vespers,
a far off rumble
tumbling amid the boulders
and crevices of hope and expectation
mimicking heartbeats like a drum,
finding in its steady voice
a crescendo of confident volume,
and plunging upon the valley
with the steel awkwardness
of Sunday morning bells
unmistakable and confident

thunderous and bold
plundering eardrums and
calendars and heresy
and no barrier, no wall, no weapon,
no language, no lie, no treasure
can stop it haunting
hunting
monstrous clamoring
singing crying dancing
devilish death.

"Alisio," Papa said. "I been a bad man. I'm gonna go to hell."

"Papa, don't talk like that. I'll call the priest."

"No, Alisio, listen. I'll confess to you. You be my priest."

"No, Pa. Please."

"You no talk. Listen. All my life I know I'm going to hell. That makes me sad. But, nothing I can do."

"Papa, don't talk like this. You're a good man. You're good to me. Maybe you've been a bad Catholic, but you're a good man. God will understand."

"I don't know about God. But, now I'm telling you. I made a sin when I was young, Alisio. Bad sin."

Papa looked defeated, conquered.

"Oh, Papa," Alisio blurted, "stop this. I don't care what you did. I love you."

It was a sudden, emotional outburst. He didn't mean to be so honest. He hadn't meant to say I love you but he'd said it, and it was done.

13

Love
it's got to tumble
into the cold stone staircase
of black granite
and cold marble stairs
fissured
like a silent pyrite vein
so that only after years of effort
can a heart break
beyond the black staircase
covered in
ink indelible love.

"Alisio," Papa Giovanni said, "come close. You be my witness. God, He listens to you. Let me confess."

Papa paused. Breaths were hard work, each one earned, like the setting of a wheel. He looked at Alisio. His eyes begged. Please, Alisio, they begged, I gave you my gun, the thing I love the most, now take my sin, the thing I hate the most.

Papa shifted his eyes, then looked again to Alisio.

"I was a young man. Just a young man, Alisio" Papa began. "Italy, she had no work, everyone fighting for each small job. Mama and me, we're poor. Mama, she made a baby. It's a boy. Nice bambino. Black hair. But we got no food. I think to myself: maybe he'll starve; maybe he'll get shot. I don't know. Maybe I'll get shot, and he starves anyway. I figure and think for two days. I think, hey, no good for this baby boy to be alive. I save him a lotta pain. I love him too much. Finally, I take that baby, and I snap his little neck. He died quick, and I tell Mama a street bullet come and killed him. Later, I made things right at confession with Father Anselmo. We made a small funeral and a strong wood box for his body. Father Anselmo prays to Our Father, and he sprinkles the holy water on the box. Then, before he says Amen, he says, `Giovanni, I condemn you and the Church condemns you; no man is forgiven for what you did.' He tells this in front of all my village, in front of Mama. Mama, she's already wearing sadness on her face. Now she must add shame. I cannot talk for the anger in my jaws, but I swear then that no man will ever bring pain to me or Mama or my family again. It was then that my heart crawled into the blackness and became as granite. But, Alisio, I love that baby all these years. I think, when I die, God He's gonna show me that little boy, then send me to hell and never see him again. I'm afraid, Alisio. I want to kiss my son. You're like my son, Alisio. So you talk to God for me. Talk with a son's heart. He'll listen."

What confession this?
Tattered bundles of fragile words
formed of shabby cloth
and thread of despicable humanity
splattered with lies like communicable stains.
Must truth hide behind such words?
Must truth cringe behind such
forbidding energy
full of ripe blood pumping

gallons of miserable failure?
Requiescat in pace
and
Ego te absolvo, Giovanni,
the almighty curtain of absolution
must engulf you
swallow you
embrace you
with arms of fire
heated to the two thousandth degree
hot enough to sear
the guilty memory from your hardened skin.
But I
I am left as if the breath
and moisture of my
mouth and lungs
were putty;
left as if two iconoclastic
balconies merged at the center of my youth
while on this side
all the world walks in peaceful walking
peaceful play
peaceful touching
peaceful groups
like grasses grown in kind
flowers grown in spring

families grown in trust,
while I
I walk the other stair
alone.

    Papa Giovanni sighed, and Alisio knew the end was upon him. Alisio cried as he called out to God's angels.

Memory Basket

_____

That morning, during the hot days and bright skies of mid-summer, Sarah held her stomach and would not allow her mother to touch her. Mary Anne took her to the doctor who ordered tests. Several weeks later, as summer neared its end, the results were analyzed, and the doctor explained the diagnosis.

"Neuroblastoma," Doctor Reed said.

"What exactly is it?" Mary Anne asked.

"It's a tumor. It often forms in the adrenal gland. It's a childhood disease. Untreated, it spreads. Sarah exhibits several late stage symptoms. The large mass in her stomach, the black and blue bruises beginning under the facial skin; also the swollen, puffy cheeks. The tests confirm that it has progressed beyond the cure stage."

"Beyond the cure stage?" Mary Anne asked. "What do you mean?"

Doctor Reed pressed his lips together and raised his eyes to express the futility of second-guessing this disease. "Sometimes these things just happen, and there is no explanation. I'm sorry." He paused to give her a little time. "We can minimize Sarah's discomfort with pain medication," he continued, "but I recommend no other treatment."

He lowered his head, and closed the file.

"She's going to die?" Mary Anne asked.

He nodded. "Within a few months," he said, as gently as he could, as gently as anyone can say a thing like that. Doctor Reed excused himself and left her alone to absorb the news.

The antiseptic room could not sterilize the frightening aloneness that filled her. Her teeth scraped together and her jaws quivered. She twisted her head in disbelief, as if this strong gesture could make the doctor's words untrue. She slammed her eyes closed and reeled in the salty colors of lightening and headache. And finally, she cried.

After some minutes, she left the room to pick up Sarah from the nursery.

Summer gave way to the fierce colors of autumn, and Mary Anne decided to return home. It was new territory for Mary Anne. She did not know how to watch a child die, and she did not like to accept help from anyone. Nevertheless, she called her father, and he agreed that they could live in Grandma Rose's old house, in order to be near the family. Mary Anne's father converted it to two apartments after Grandma Rose died. That's how they ended up at Grandma Rose's.

When the first winter cold front arrived, the furnace didn't work. They went down to the basement to look at it. In the summers of her youth, Mary Anne loved the smell of the dark slate walls, full of moisture and algae. But the winter basement was different -- solitary, frigid, uninviting. The furnace sat at the far corner, where the coal bin used to be. It was beige, new, covered with recent dust, without history or heat.

Mary Anne walked around the furnace. She attempted no repair, but she did chant, "Damn you. Damn you," in an attempt to engender both fear and guilt in the soul of the thing, but the furnace made no response.

Sarah explored. While looking through some boxes, she found an old wooden picnic basket. It looked like an ordinary brown woven basket with a round handle wrapped with a strand of wicker and two small hinges which let the top open and close, but Mary Anne shrieked when her daughter lifted it from the cardboard box. She shrieked with that loss of breath caused from too much stimuli too soon coming. There was the basket and there were the memories. Come on Grandma, what's going on here?

"What is it?" asked Sarah.

"That basket. Grandma Rose's memory basket."

Sarah looked puzzled.

Mary Anne touched the basket. She and Sarah both held it.

"Grandma Rose kept it in the dining room, on top of the linen chest," Mary Anne said. Her voice softened with the pictures popping through her head. "On Christmas eve it was full of popcorn balls, wrapped in green and red cellophane. And every Easter Sunday it had jelly beans and those little yellow marshmallow chickens. You know the ones with the tiny black eyes?"

She smiled as she spoke. Mary Anne loved those chicks. She'd bite the heads and pull with her teeth, and Grandma Rose would smile at the sticky strings of white marshmallow that clung to Mary Anne's cheek, and she would kiss them off Mary Anne's face with loud kisses, and tell the aunts, "The only way to wash your favorite grand-daughter's face is with kisses."

"Why did she put candy in the basket?" Sarah wanted to know.

"To remind her to make memories," Mary Anne said.

"Make memories?"

"That's how she talked. Every Christmas when I was little she put popcorn balls in there. Whenever I visited, we'd do things, you know, like spy on the moon to see if Santa would fly by. She would push the big rocking chair to the window in the living room, and then I would jump on her lap. While we spied on the moon, we ate the popcorn balls. And we made a memory."

"So the memory basket made memories?"

"Well, I guess in a way. But it was more than that for Grandma Rose. It was almost as if it had a life of its own for her."

"Why, mom? What do you mean?"

Although the house was cold, and Mary Anne was worried about Sarah, and herself for that matter, she sat on the bottom tread of the narrow basement stairs and decided that maybe by talking the cold would diminish, especially since she still had no idea how to get the furnace started.

"Grandma Rose told me the story of her basket. If you like, I'll tell you."

"All right," Sarah said. She placed the old basket in front of her mother and sat on it.

"Grandma Rose left Italy right after she was married. She loved her mother very much and her mother loved her, but they both knew that they would not see each other again. When it was time to get on the boat, Grandma Rose's mother handed her the basket. `Here,' she said to her. `Take this basket. It has apples and cheese. Also, some bread. I made the bread. The food is for the trip. After the food is gone, you keep the basket, and whenever you want, you have the basket to remember me. It's your memory basket. As long as you have it, my memory is alive.'

"Grandma and her mother cried and hugged and said I love you and Grandma got on the boat and never saw her mother again. She used to say, `With memories, no one really dies.'"

Mary Anne stopped a moment. Her mind released images of her own memories of Grandma Rose, picking out dusty chunks of coal from the sooty coal box, or helping her can tomatoes, and how she reached way up to put the jars on those shelves back in the corner near the window, nailed shut to keep the cold out. But she knew this was not the time to reminisce. She re-focused her eyes in the present.

"How does it work?" Sarah wanted to know.

"It doesn't work. It's just a basket. You sort of pretend."

"You pretend the memories?"

"No, Sarah. Not like that. The memories are real. It's just . . ." How do you explain it? As she searched for an answer, Sarah spoke.

"It's like magic. Huh, mom? When you see the basket you think of Grandma Rose. Just like when she saw it she thought of her mom."

"Yes. Like that," Mary Anne agreed.

"Do you have to give it away to make it work? Like Grandma Rose's mom, or does it count that we found it?"

"It can count for us, but we won't lose it any more."

The cold had increased, and Mary Anne remembered back to her childhood when Grandma Rose would light the oven to heat the kitchen on chilly winter mornings.

"Let's go upstairs and get warm," she said.

Mary Anne pushed a kitchen chair around to face the stove. She turned the knob for the top front burner, and a round, blue flame appeared with jitterbug red tips.

"Ah, we have gas," she said. Then she turned on the remaining burners, set the oven at 400 degrees and opened the door.

"An old trick Grandma used when I was growing up," she said. "The stove will heat the room, and we can both get warm. You sit down, and I'll call a furnace repair shop."

Mary Anne dialed the number. As it rang, she remembered cold winter mornings, before the house warmed up, Grandma Rose would turn the burners on to "Chase the chill out." It was almost a whisper, but Mary Anne thought she heard Grandma Rose's voice telling her to "Sit down and have some toast and cocoa before you go to school. I'll turn on the burners to chase the chill out."

The secretary told Mary Anne that someone would be there in half an hour. He made it in less than twenty minutes. The kitchen was warm by then, and Mary Anne pointed him toward the basement. He was tall, and Mary Anne thought he looked handsome in spite of the ugly blue sailor's cap he had pulled over his ears. She felt uncomfortable thinking about handsome furnace repairmen when she sensed another almost inaudible whisper from Grandma Rose. "He's a handsome boy, make him some cocoa and cinnamon toast."

"Don't start with me, Grandma," Mary Anne said out loud.

"What do you mean, mommy?" Sarah asked.

Mary Anne realized she had spoken her thought. "Oh, nothing, Sarah. I was just thinking about something." To herself she said, thank God that man is downstairs and didn't hear me talking to myself. She turned toward the cellar.

"You wait here, Sarah. We'll be right up."

The repairman stretched out on the damp floor. He leaned on one elbow and breathed on his finger tips.

"We're in luck," he said. "The pilot light went out. I just re-lit it. In a minute this thing should heat right up."

Mary Anne felt uneasy and charmed at the same time. His smile was friendly and his eyes dreamy. But I hate that hat, she corrected her thoughts, and I'm not getting involved. I've got my daughter to consider.

The repairman sat up, and rubbed his hands together. As he did, the furnace ignited, and the smooth, oiled sound of the motor filled the basement.

"You'll have heat soon," he said. He picked up his tools and walked up the steps.

"Did you fix it?" Sarah asked.

"Sure I did."

"I knew you would. Thank you."

"Yes," Mary Anne said. "Thank you."

"No problem. Give us a call if you need us again."

He left, and Mary Anne felt a small desire to call him back, but that would require some commitment, and she had no time for that. She closed the door and returned to the table. She left the oven on to give the house time to heat up. Then, the desire came upon her for food.

"We need hot cocoa and toast," she said. "Would you like to make hot cocoa and toast, Sarah?"

"Yes," she said.

"With cinnamon on the toast?" Mary Anne asked.

"Cinnamon?"

Before she could prevent herself from thinking

it, she thought, did you put us up to this? Oh, God, she thought, now I'm accusing my dead grandmother of tricking me into wanting cinnamon toast.

"Sure," she said. "Cinnamon toast. Goes great with cocoa."

She stood and opened two lower cabinet doors. She found a pan. "You get the milk," she said, "while I find the cinnamon."

Sarah got the milk and the cocoa. Mary Anne let her pour the milk into the pan and stir in the cocoa with a maplewood spoon. As she stirred the cocoa, an interested expression surfaced on her bruised face.

"Are we making a memory?" Sarah asked.

Mary Anne paused.

"You know, like Grandma Rose's memory basket," Sarah added.

"I guess we are," her mother said. "I guess we are."

They sipped the steamy warmth of the cocoa. They chewed the buttery honey-sugar cinnamon bread. The stove and the furnace heated the room. They undid their hats and coats, and as Mary Anne relaxed, she found herself wondering what that repairman kisses like. As quickly as she wondered it, she scolded her grandmother. Don't do that to me, Grandma, she said.

But the feeling held, and Sarah smiled, and the house was warm, and for a while Mary Anne felt safe.

An hour later, Mary Anne put Sarah to bed. She clicked the safety bars of the hospital bed into place and kissed Sarah on the nose.

She walked to the living room and sat down

in the old rocking chair. She closed her eyes, and enjoyed the calmness punctuated by the monotony of motion and the rocker's secure squeak. It reminded Mary Anne of the times she sat with Grandma Rose, wrapped between her abundant breasts and her flabby arms, smelling the garlic and oregano on her apron. She considered the earlier urge to experiment with kissing the repairman, and grinned as she recalled the first of several conversations with Grandma Rose regarding kissing.

It was summer, the night heat aggressive with humidity, Mary Anne out of breath with secrets.

"Tonight I kissed Kevin O'Hanley," she told Grandma Rose.

"You did?"

"Is that bad?"

"I don't know," Grandma Rose answered. "I've never kissed an Irishman."

With that memory fresh, like moisture for her mind, she asked Grandma Rose, "What do you think about me kissing a furnace repairman?" Although Grandma Rose did not answer, Mary Anne decided that it might be worth investigating some day. What would she do when Sarah was gone? About men? About everything? She did not want to struggle with those questions too long. They were heavy questions, ponderous and dangerous. She was frightened enough. She would worry about the future later.

The questions refused to rest quietly, and often they whirled into her mind, like a sudden cold wind. Mary Anne pushed them back into the blackness at the root of her head, where they remained, hibernating. The winter snow arrived, and for several long weeks the weather was unkind, the sky gray, the wind fierce.

Mary Anne began to feel guilty for any time she spent away from Sarah, because she reasoned that all of her time should be devoted to her. Sometimes she wished for a friend, someone she could talk to, someone who would not judge her for the selfish desires she had for romance, someone who would understand the frustration of caring for a child who was dying, the agony of not knowing how much time was left. She did not want to lose her baby but she was going away and there was nothing anyone could do, nothing she could do. She inhaled with short stuttered breaths. She wanted to explain, wanted someone to comprehend. Sometimes she ached for someone to hold her.

"Why is she going to die?" she whispered. Even Grandma Rose had no answer.

Suddenly, Sarah marched into the room, displaying a white-bandaged doll wrapped in a blanket, propped into a sitting position against the short side of Grandma Rose's basket.

"Look," Sarah said. "How do you like dolly's new bed?"

"Grandma Rose's basket?" Mary Anne asked in surprise. "Dolly's bed?"

"Yes. It has high sides and handles like mine, so it's safe. Besides, it's special."

"I don't know, Sarah."

Sarah placed the basket on the floor, and crossed her arms. She spoke with sternness and with the force of a young girl's unchangeable determination.

"Mom, it's perfect. Grandma Rose sent it to us." She pointed to the basket-turned-doll's-bed. "She's not dead anymore. She gave the basket to you. Now you can give it to me. And besides, it's perfect for dolly."

Sarah tilted her head slightly to the right. She puckered her lips, but the swelling prevented a pout. What she got was a frown with her tongue sticking from the side of her mouth.

"Please, mom?"

It made Mary Anne laugh. "Oh, all right," she said. "Get out of here."

Sarah nodded, snapped up the basket-turned-hospital-bed, and marched, almost militarily, from the room.

"I owe her so much . . ." Mary Anne didn't finish with words. Her face muscles tightened. She opened her hand, palm up, as if the explanation she needed were etched in the lines.

Sarah grew weaker. Occasionally, she seemed to perk up and she wanted to play with the nurse dolly, and once, she asked Mary Anne to rock her by the window so she could watch the moon. The winter dragged on, bleak and patient, with days of calm and days of wind which made the tree branches sound like the crying of a granite conch.

That next Saturday, the outside temperature took a rare mid-winter jump into the high thirties, one of those prophetic reminders that spring will eventually change things. The change in temperature thawed the dry snow and made it great for packing.

Mary Anne folded laundry while Sarah napped. The sun broke through the high white clouds and its sudden appearance through the window brightened the room. Mary Anne looked out on the naked, black forms of the trees. At several different branches, small mounds of snow sat like birds' nests; they almost looked warm. Mary Anne decided to play in the snow. She pushed the laundry basket away from her legs and went to the closet for a hooded sweater, a coat, a scarf, and gloves.

She walked off the back porch, and watched the melting snow on the window. Tiny ice pieces slid down the glass, leaving shiny, reflective trails.

Mary Anne walked into the yard. She bent down and grabbed an armload of snow. She packed it together and began to roll it into a ball. When it was about the size of a snowman's belly, she packed handsful of snow around the base and smoothed the rough edges of the ball with circular strokes. Smokey breath coiled from her throat, full of muscle and frosty life.

She rolled a second ball and lifted it onto the base. Again, she packed snow, like mortar, where the two balls met, and again she smoothed the rough edges with circular strokes, making it right, making it perfect. Finally, she rolled a ball the size of a 10-quart pot. She placed it on the top of her snowman and packed it into place.

She moved close to the snowman and looked directly at the head. She straightened her finger to use as a chisel, and she began to carve the face. Tiny strokes at first; a quick curl for one eyebrow, then the other. She made a nose, but it was too thin, so she added more to the sides. She studied the face, and worked again with swift movements to create delicate eyes, a proud nose, and a mouth that smiled without lips. She couldn't figure out how to make lips.

She was lost in the dream of creating the imaginary person with the snowman face. The sun continued to shine bright, even as it settled against the horizon. For a while time stopped, and Mary Anne, with every handful of memory she could hold, tried to chisel the face of her grandmother into the snow creature. Finally, when she realized what she was trying to do, she could not continue. She sat in the snow and leaned against the snowman.

She inhaled the cold air, and she felt the fear of losing Sarah deep in her chest, burning breaths so cold she visualized the lining of her lungs freezing in deadly patterns of lace. The hot vapor of her breath portioned between her teeth and out her nostrils like visible drum beats. She pounded the snow at her side and lifted her hand to her face. The glove was cold and bits of snow scratched her skin. Her cheeks burned with chill and anger. She kicked and screamed. Then, depleted, she cried. She cried for being happy. She cried for being sad. She cried because she had carried herself and her fears and the dangers of living for too long alone. And realizing this, she stopped abruptly. Whether it was the realization of her own emotion or the intuition of motherhood, she could not say, but she became immediately aware of Sarah.

"What's the matter, mom?" Sarah called to her.

Like antennae, Mary Anne's ears and eyes sought Sarah. "Oh, God, what?" She jumped to her feet and ran to the porch. Sarah stood in her clothes and slippers, no coat, no hat, shivering and smiling.

"Did you make that snowman?" she asked.

"Sarah, what are you doing outside? My God, what are you thinking? Get in the house," Mary Anne said. She reached for Sarah and lifted her. She weighed little more than the clothes she wore.

Once inside, small beads of sweat rose on Sarah's face. She was excited by her mother's snowman, and she giggled like a muffin-girl as Mary Anne carried her to her room. But exhaustion began to grip her.

Mary Anne removed the cold clothes and dressed Sarah in thick flannel pajamas with a pattern of tumbling circus clowns. As she buttoned the top, Mary Anne wondered how many more times she would get to dress her baby. Then she hugged Sarah and held her with both arms.

Sarah, resting against Mary Anne, closed her eyes and made no more effort to play. "I don't hurt anywhere, mom," Sarah said. The discoloration around her eyes turned slightly luminescent, almost purple. She lifted her shoulders as if the muscles of her lungs required help, and she took small, shallow breaths.

"You need to go to bed now," Mary Anne said.

Sarah asked for the hospital doll. Mary Anne gave it to her, and tucked the blankets around them both. Sarah closed her eyes.

Mary Anne decided against a long bath. She

would be luxurious some other time. She washed, changed into dry clothes, and returned to Sarah's room.

She leaned against the doorway of Grandma Rose's old bedroom. The ornate mahogany door trim had scars, scratches from who knows what. The painters had put two coats of white latex paint over the wood, but somehow the oldness of it remained, like a pulse. Sarah struggled with her breaths, and she pulled the doll against her cheek. Mary Anne heard a rustle. Grandma? she asked. But when she turned, she realized that it was merely the creaking of an old house. Funny, she thought, how silence can be so full of little noises. Sarah inhaled unevenly, as if phlegm blocked her nose and her tongue was too thick for her mouth. Mary Anne stood straighter, and instinctively lifted her arms toward the bed. But her expectant hands remained empty. There was nothing for them to do. She sighed.

The noise woke Sarah. "Mom?" she asked. Her voice weighed little.

Mary Anne moved to the side of the bed. Sarah pointed at the hospital tray.

"Put dolly in the basket," she said.

Mary Anne placed the dolly safely within the wicker.

Sarah pulled the blankets up to her chin. She smiled at her mother. Her fingers held the sheet, and her breathing remained difficult and forced. Her eyes did not blink, but Mary Anne thought they moved a little under the lids.

Mary Anne clutched the basket, not daring to manufacture words out of her feelings. She leaned into the door casing and felt the memory of her grandmother's arms, plump and comfortable. She thought she heard Grandma Rose humming a lullaby, but this time she did not scold her. She stared at her daughter, waiting.

A Deepening Heart

_____

Often, during times of desperation, only his love for Miss Agnes Perser kept Nathan Branchwell on the right side of sanity, and one day, the Rev. Perser would give permission for Nathan to marry her. The more he missed Agnes, the more Nathan wished for the Civil War to end. The men had gone nearly five months without pay. Rations arrived with little regularity, and the soldiers began to spend more of their time and ammunition on rabbit and squirrel than on battle. Uniforms became torn, unwashed, and often devoid of rank or insignia. The men simply knew by face who was private, who was sergeant. This was the general condition of the men of the 110th Pennsylvania on the night of October 19th, 1864. They had been camped nearly four weeks near Kernstown, Virginia, and Nathan sat alone watching the jittery flametips of his fire. The quiet of darkness settled over him, and his thoughts slipped unexpectedly into a peacefulness he had not dared in years. The gurgle of the stream and the soft breeze rustling the grass soothed him. His breathing felt liquid and transparent, as if he were connected to the currents of water and the currents of air, and all the simple breaths he breathed reminded him of life and of growing things like hay and sunflowers in a garden.

Nathan reached the decision to join the volunteers after he spoke with the Reverend.

"I want to marry Miss Agnes," he said to Rev. Perser.

"I can't allow it," the Reverend said.

"Why not?"

"It's the time, my boy. War. Uncertainty. I want my daughter to enjoy a comfortable home. You have no stake, Nathan. Nothing to offer."

"What can I do?"

"I don't know."

They stood quiet a moment. Then the Reverend mused. "Men honor gold," he said. "Whatever should happen, gold will last."

"Some men find their fortunes in war."

"Some men do, yes."

"I will."

Reverend Perser studied him.

"Please, sir."

"I cannot make such a decision for you, Nathan, but if you return from the war with gold enough to stock a young farm, I believe the good Lord will bless your efforts. With that, I would grant a union between you and my daughter."

Nathan accepted his admonition, and of those

irregular times when the soldiers did receive their thirteen dollars in monthly pay, he traded his paper money for gold. He offered three times the face value of any gold coin. It was a time of general madness, so his mild idiosyncrasy caused little concern, and men sought him out, for three times the money meant three times the whiskey and sometimes a woman's favor. Over a period of three and a half years, Nathan traded for and saved two hundred dollars, four 50-dollar gold pieces.

How much would two hundred dollars buy at the end of the war? Nathan felt certain he could afford one milk cow, two Morgan horses, a double harness and a plow, a shovel, a hay fork, and all the seed for a first planting of beans, corn, and hay. Besides these he added a double-handled saw and two axes, one chopping and one finishing, so he could fell the trees and shape them into a two-room cabin. He was certain to find a down mattress, pots, kitchen utensils, and such cooking provisions as flour, lard, and salt to last the first year. Finally, with good neighbors, he would stand a barn of a weekend, pen in some chickens, fence in a hog, and still manage to bury two of the gold coins. Surely, the Reverend would honor his promise.

Suddenly, the gallop of a horse disturbed Nathan's reverie. He watched the rider kick the sides of the animal all the way to the Captain's tent. This bothered Nathan, because he respected animals, and he liked them. Since he cared for the stock, Nathan knew the horse would be lathered and sore and he would be up late caring for it.

Captain Hollingsworth jumped from his chair,

and the rider saluted. Nathan watched the men gesture, their arms and heads bobbing shadowy behind the glow of the Captain's fire. What news did this night rider bring?

Captain Hollingsworth commanded the 110th Pennsylvania. He had not distinguished himself in battle, but he courted power, and his commander, Colonel Geoffrey MacGeorge, was a man who remembered favors. Captain Hollingsworth spent much time cultivating the Colonel's ear, hoping that at war's end, the Colonel would reward him with the rank of Major. The Captain suspected that Washington and Richmond were close to resolving their differences, and he knew he needed one last opportunity to impress the colonel.

In the morning, word spread: a major battle, a decisive battle, perhaps a concluding battle threatened. No one knew specifics, but the rumors of war bring tension, and weary expectation mingled with coffee and talk.

Captain Hollingsworth called for the tracker, Manning, two sharpshooters, Steadman and French, and Nathan.

"Men, Colonel Mac George has put me in charge of a scouting party. We won't engage, just survey. I have a sense he'll reward any good news we bring him." Then he turned to Nathan. "Branchwell, I want you along to watch the stock in case of an injury. They must be ready for quick rides and hard terrain."

"What are we looking for, sir?" Manning asked.

"I don't know. And I don't know what we'll find." Before he dismissed them, he said, "Gather gear and supplies. We leave in two hours."

They took a southern tack, using the protection of forests along the hills. Late on the second afternoon, they rode into a tree line where the air turned pungent.

"What's that smell?"

"Quiet," Hollingsworth said.

They slowed their pace, but the horses struggled against the reins. The men heard no unusual sound, but their ears strained in an effort to interpret the uneasiness they felt. Suddenly, they all stopped. Ahead of them, through the branches and leaves, they saw a battlefield, a small, unknown location, quiet and eerie with motionlessness. Captain Hollingsworth dismounted. He handed the reins to Nathan. The captain signaled the others to follow him. Each, in turn, slipped from the saddle and gave their reins to Nathan. Nathan pulled the horses together behind a tree.

"Shhhh. Shhhhhhh," he whispered.

The tree line followed the contour of the hillside opening to a small clearing with a stream which flowed away from them. Each man took a position crouched behind a tree. They waited, listening, watching for movement. Nathan kept the animals quiet, but they didn't like the acrid smell.

Manning circled left for half an hour. He found no signs of life. Captain Hollingsworth panned the field with his looking glass again and again. Finally, he decided the meadow contained no threat, and he ordered the men out of the trees. Their senses remained alert, but even for these men who had come to know depravity, the stench and silence of this dead place restrained them. Their voices fell momentarily dry, like talcum. Death stretched before them without end. In the heat, bloated carrion stunk like vinegar. Cannons lay muzzle first into the mud. Ghostly bodies leaned as if asleep, and no one could distinguish blue uniform from gray. Their ears began to fill with a quiet buzz of flies -- blowflies, horseflies, and blackflies, and at once the men recognized that the gray film which dulled the red earth was alive. They watched the hypnotic undulation of maggoty decay. Nathan huddled within the hot breath of the horses, and although flies found their salty hides, the horses, knowing Nathan, stayed calm. Minutes dragged with the miserable slowness of the sun, and nothing stirred -- not squirrel, not rabbit, not man.

Hollingsworth turned his thoughts to the Colonel. How would he react to this event? It seemed final, as no battle before had felt. Hollingsworth knew he would have to find something exemplary for his report, but nothing exemplary remained among the carnage, only the pitiful silence of exhausted savagery.

Suddenly, a mule brayed. When they heard it, each man strained to determine its origin. Again, the pathetic bray sounded, painful and unhappy, and with it the sucking sound of a boot or a foot or a hoof pulling against mud.

"There," Nathan shouted, and he ran the twenty yards, jumping over cadavers and splintered trees to a muddy bank. The others followed to a low gully, the slow running water in its basin stained purple. A Confederate stamp on the mule's strap identified it. The mule looked young, recently pressed into service. The wide black eyes of the beast looked full of puzzlement.

"Help me get it to its feet," Nathan said.

"Wait," Captain Hollingsworth said. "It's a Reb. Leave it be."

"It's a mule," Nathan said.

"It's a Reb mule," the captain repeated.

"Let me save it."

Nathan reached for the rein and tugged, but the brute could only show its teeth and bray. Nathan struggled, but mud and exhaustion held the beast, and it would not stand. Nathan turned to the others. "Help me," he said.

Steadman and French moved to help.

"Stop," Hollingsworth said. "I said it's a Reb, and a Reb it stays." He drew his side arm and cocked the lever.

"It's not our enemy, Captain. It's a mule, a live thing among all this dead."

"That's dangerous talk, Branchwell. You should know better."

Hollingsworth pointed his pistol at the aggrieved animal, but Nathan stepped between them.

"I can't let you, sir. I can't."

"Don't make me shoot you over a dumb Reb mule. Step aside."

Nathan looked squarely into his commander's eyes. The Captain did not blink.

"I'm asking you not to shoot it," Nathan said.

"You or the mule," Hollingsworth replied.

Nathan clenched his teeth and decided to back away. As he took a step, Hollingsworth fired, and Nathan jumped. The bullet missed Nathan, but dirt sprayed onto his boots.

"Sir," French called. "Are you sure this is what you want?"

"He disobeyed an order."

"But, sir, it's Branchwell."

Nathan's nose flared, and he kept his eyes on the trickle of smoke that eased from the barrel of Hollingsworth's Colt. For a moment, no one spoke.

Finally, Hollingsworth said, "Mount up. There's nothing to report here."

Nathan did not move. "What about the mule?"

Hollingsworth walked toward the horses. "Mount up," he said. As he swung into the saddle, he looked at French. "Shoot the Reb."

"Wait," Nathan said. "I'll pay."

Hollingsworth reined his horse.

"There are four of you. I've saved four fifty-dollar gold pieces. If you help me with this mule and let me take him home, I'll give them to you. One for each."

"I'll take a gold piece over a dead mule any day," French said. "What's the loss if one Reb mule lives?"

Hollingsworth dismounted and nodded his chin in the direction of the mule.

Nathan leaned down and grabbed the mule's reins. The mule curled its lip, braying and jerking its head. Steadman and French pushed the haunches, forcing the animal to stand. Gray mud oozed under the shifted weight. A dank pool of dark water filled the hollow left by the emaciated body. Nathan motioned with his eyes, and Steadman unstrapped the broken supply baskets from the mule's back, leaving the tie straps. Nathan held the reins and whispered to it.

"Calm now. Calm," he said.

Manning pulled one hoof from the glue-like mud, and French pushed. The frightened mule lifted one leg, then another. Finally, it stood on firm ground.

Nathan found a wound at its rear leg near the stomach. He thought the lead might have grazed the flesh and not entered it.

"It's free," Hollingsworth said. "Pay us."

Nathan examined their greedy eyes. As he reached for his pouch, he realized the cost of this mule -- his gold, his farm, perhaps even his marriage. He could not renege. Even if he shot the mule himself, the others would take his gold. A battlefield oath cannot be undone.

The pouch felt heavy and full of promise. As he drew the strings apart, the men moved closer, every eye on the coins. One at a time, he paid their fee: Hollingsworth, Manning, Steadman, and French.

Nathan kept his original enlistment orders at the bottom of the pouch. After handing over the last gold piece, he removed the paper. It was creased and yellowed, but he had preserved it all these long years. To his own surprise, he tore the paper into small pieces and let them drop around his feet.

"We're done with this war," he said. He pulled the reins to lead the mule. "We're going home."

He moved to the horses, untied his haversack, grabbed his musket, and walked away. He headed north in search of water and perhaps some rest. He did not say good-bye, nor did he flinch when Hollingsworth called after him. Instead, he wondered if Miss Agnes Perser would consider one rebel mule wealth enough for marriage if the man who possessed it loved her.

The sun turned okra, and a thin twilight fog began to form. Nathan coaxed the mule with soft encouragement, even though the stout neck sagged and the eyes began to lose their glisten. Nathan tried to comfort the animal by rubbing its jaw and feeding it a hard-tack cracker. The wound bled again, but not seriously, Nathan judged. Still, a bleeding wound stirs concern. After perhaps two hours, he stopped at the top of a hill. They had traveled far enough from the slaughter to smell pine pitch, and the water in the stream ran clear over bluestone and pebbles. He could see the battlefield, but from a distance. The distance gave him courage enough to ignore it and to begin what might be called a healing as reality moved slightly toward memory.

They walked down into a green gully to camp. Nathan tied the reins to a rope, and he tied the rope to a tree so the animal could graze. The mule stood silent, as if it still carried supply boxes and it hadn't slept in a day or two.

Nathan boiled water for coffee. He did not eat. He rubbed his hands in the fire's warmth, and he wondered about the value of the mule, the gold it cost, and the queer decision to forsake the war. He imagined the conversation with his father. His father would say, "Brute appearance calls it foolhardy, but in ten years you'll know its value." Then Nathan imagined his father would return to his field work. Perhaps he would never speak of it again.

The loss of gold seemed fundamentally unsound. But what price a life? His mother, he knew, would value the life. Comfort, to her, came in a smile and a thankful embrace. She would be happy that Nathan returned home alive. Whether he returned with gold or with a mule she wouldn't care. But that's a mother's love; it holds no count in the business of men.

A breeze rustled the weeds, and Nathan finished the coffee with a gulp. He felt tired, and he began to ache in the way only a man who has escaped war can ache, bone-deep and permanent. He thought how the end of this journey would bring him home. Then he closed his eyes. He imagined that his father would stop his work to watch Nathan's approach. His mother would smile and wave and call his name. And he would see Agnes. As he thought of them together, he slept nearly four hours without waking.

When he did awaken, it took several seconds before he remembered where he was and why. He turned to see the mule in the moonlight. He stirred the coals of the campfire, added broken twigs, and coaxed the weary embers back to flame. He went to the mule and stroked its mud-caked hide. "I'll rinse you in the daylight," he said. He looked across the back of the mule to the hill-line admiring the calm of the night-lit tips of high grass. It was the first time since leaving home he was alone. The mule brayed. The fire crackled. The night solitude carried the noises in echoes. He went to his bedroll and made a pipe.

The mule moved a little closer to the tree, but Nathan could not tell if it had grazed. Come light, he would hand feed it and bring it to the water for drink. Then he would wash the mud from it to begin its rejuvenation. He planned his route north, almost a straight walk, barring renegade militia and federal search parties. He would walk slow, stopping to rest the mule. He might need to work a day at a willing farm for food. Even under the worst scenario, he calculated he'd be home in three weeks. The thought of it made him smile. Home. Home and Agnes.

He slept again.

At dawn, the mule brayed and woke him. Nathan took the mule's bray as a good sign; perhaps it wanted water or feed. While the sun moved along the horizon, Nathan rose to attend the mule. He undid the rope to lead the animal to the stream. It brayed again, but Nathan shivered at the sorrowful sound.

"What?" he said to it, touching the jaw, patting the haunch. The eyes looked hollow and dry, beginning to turn opaque around the edges.

"You'll be fine," Nathan said. "Come on."

He tugged the rein. The mule trudged to water's edge without resistance, its ribs shadowy beneath its hide. It did not bend to drink. Nathan cupped a handful of water and rubbed it around the beast's lips and tongue. Droplets fell from its whiskers back into the stream, and the mule bent after them to drink.

Nathan patted its neck. "Good," he said.

Nathan bent too and rinsed his mouth. Then he drank.

He brought the mule to grass and left it untied; it would not run. He went to the fire and added kindling and pinecones to the embers. He sat in the dewy sunrise, the smoke from the campfire a comfort of pine scent and ash. The mule moved warily to graze and chewed the grass more like a cow making cud than a horse-breed chewing feed, slow and repetitive, almost melancholic. He thought the mule looked haggard. Perhaps the emotion of the battlefield kept him from recognizing the mule's state. Could it have been his frustration with death that led him to the reckless choice he now possessed? Why did he save the animal? Why did he pay such an awful price for its life? Surly, Agnes would ask him these very questions.

"Why, Nathan? What drove you?" she might ask.

He knew what he would tell her. One thing only drove him. Love. It felt like an incorrigible piece of knowledge, yet true and agreeable, like his love for her. He had to save the beast. It had survived the war, and Nathan knew it represented both his own survival and the survival of their love. That's what he would tell Agnes. He looked upon the sad, silent beast, and in that moment, he loved it -- as a symbol, as a living thing, as a hope. Nathan drew on his pipe and exhaled a firm stream of smoke. He poured coffee into the metal cup and sipped gingerly allowing the heat and sour grounds to ease past his tongue. The warmth seeped into his stomach, and the heat of his belly and the heat of the cup against his hands warmed him.

The Rev. Perser would also ask Nathan about his decision. Rev. Perser was a man of principles, a godly man, a man obligated to rigid rules -- the singular moralities of Christian faith and the simple exigency of money in a commercial economy. Would he accept love as an item of barter?

"Perhaps not," Nathan answered. "What then?" he asked into the steam of the cup. But he had no answer to that. Many rules die in war, and traditions too, but a daughter's responsibility to obey her father does not die. If Rev. Perser forbade Agnes's marriage because Nathan had no money, she would obey. What then would Nathan do?

The sun began to heat the air, and Nathan decided to break camp. Perhaps an answer would come to him. He doused the fire with the remaining coffee and took the pot and his cup to the stream to rinse them. He led the mule by the rope. After he washed the utensils, he drank again and splashed his face. When he rubbed his eyes clear, he realized the mule had not moved. Nathan went to it then and coaxed it to the edge of the water, but the mule struggled and halted at the mossy recession of the bank. Nathan noticed the wound was bleeding again. He pulled the reluctant animal into the stream, and the water flowed around their legs in swirls. Nathan drenched his shirt and wiped the animal's wound clean. Then he washed the beast from head to haunch, dripping water back into the stream from its back and its legs. He cupped water to the mule's mouth and the wounded creature licked at it with its thick tongue, but it would not lower its head to drink on its own. It shook its muscles to remove the water from its hide, and droplets splashed Nathan's face and arms.

Nathan felt refreshed, almost invigorated. The chilly water cooled his skin and blood rushed pink under it. The mule stood in patient silence.

"All right, mule," Nathan said. "You're clean now. We can move on."

It's not a good idea to hike with wet feet inside wet boots, but Nathan suffered an urge to keep moving.

They progressed with slow steps, the sun ahead of them as they traveled easterly and north with the stream. The mule began to limp noticeably, and Nathan's feet began to rub against the sides of his boots.

"My toes are wrinkling," he said out loud. "We better make camp early."

He found a small area of brush and fallen leaves. Ferns and dark green bushes with tiny, white, star-shaped flowers made the place look restful. The stream hit a series of rocks and a slight drop in elevation caused the falling water to add a melody of comfort to the site. Nathan found a fire-site near two trees and a lichen-sided boulder.

He led the mule to some long grasses, but it did not eat. Nathan unstrapped the haversack and the Springfield. He took a paper plug and a pellet from the leather shot bag and loaded the musket.

"You might not be hungry," he said to the mule, "but I am. And I'm going to eat."

He patted the ribcage above the bleeding wound, turned, and walked into the trees to scare up dinner. The afternoon heat felt good on his tired muscles. He knew that the sun and a fire would dry his socks and his boots if he found dinner quickly. He came upon a decaying log, and when he kicked it, a rabbit jumped from underneath. Nathan fired quickly. The rabbit flipped once and dropped.

He lit the fire, skinned the rabbit and put it on a stick to let it skewer. He stretched his socks on a smooth stone and hung his boots upside down on two sticks.

He went to the mule. Its long ears hung like melting wax and its stubborn head fell, subdued.

51

"I'm sorry you got shot, mule."

He patted its neck. As he did, the scent of sizzling rabbit wafted into his nose. He inhaled deeply, allowing the green woods and the leaf mulch and the rabbit oil to fill his head.

"Some things are supposed to die, like that rabbit, so I can eat," he said. He grabbed the mule's ears, one in each hand. "And some things are supposed to live because they mean something. And you mean something. Do you hear?"

Nathan left the mule and strode to the fire. The tension in his stomach increased, but he confused uneasiness with hunger. He took some of the white corn meal from the flour sack, mixed water into it, and flattened the dough onto a fry pan.

"A corncake will taste good with rabbit."

Nathan turned the rabbit. Then he decided to turn his socks. They were beginning to dry, but the toes were stiff from the mud, so he had to rinse them again. He twisted each one, shook them, and replaced them on the warm stone. The corncake began to fry around the edges, and the rough doughy smell began to sweeten. He set the coffee pot to boil, and lit a pipe. He took a deep inhale and released the smoke up and away from his face. As he did so, a mosquito bit his skin and he slapped it and killed it. Its engorged belly splattered red. "Blood for blood," Nathan said and took his pipe again.

The comfort of the moment led his thoughts to Agnes, and he smiled. Somehow, he felt that she would understand his choice as a predilection in favor of life. He closed his eyes to see her, and she appeared as if real. Her long auburn hair surrounded her face and hung across both shoulders, straight and shiny like water. Her brown eyes sparkled when she smiled, and he could see in them the fond yearning and youthful hopefulness that kept Nathan human during the muddy years of war.

"Will you marry me?" he asked.

"Will you marry me, Miss Agnes?"

"Agnes, will you marry me?"

He practiced the proposal so that when he asked in person she would have to say yes.

But the practice turned bitter as he imagined Agnes hesitating. "My father . . ."

The image collapsed, and Nathan opened his eyes to the hazy beginning of sunset and coffee boiling out of the pot. He pulled the pot away from the fire, shook the fry pan and leaned the rabbit higher to let the heat cook the inside meat more thoroughly.

Nathan tapped the ashes from his pipe, then poured hot coffee into his tin cup. He lifted a twig from the fire to re-light the pipe when the mule brayed. Nathan turned his head in time to watch the mule collapse awkwardly like a dog sitting on its own tail. He dropped the stick, put his pipe on the ground, and ran to the mule. Its legs had crumpled under its body, and its great head looked forlorn. Harsh breaths snorted from its nostrils. Blood oozed from the tiny wound at its side.

"You're going to die, aren't you?" Nathan said. He sat near its head and watched the ribs swell and fall in hard cadence.

"I can't save you, but you know I tried."

Nathan looked away from the mule.

"I can't do anything more," he said, his head still turned away from the great, round eye of the beast. When he turned back to the mule, Nathan realized suddenly that the long, black eyelashes made the thing look human, as if the eyes themselves could plead. Nathan exhaled. "I suppose there is one more thing I can do," he said. "I can make your passing easier."

Nathan went to his gear and brought the Colt .44 to the mule.

Nathan insisted that killing the mule constituted an act of love, an act internal and correct, a pitiful act of kindness in a harsh time -- for where is the essence of a man if not in his capacity to love? He put the barrel into the mule's sad ear. "I love you," he whispered, and pulled the trigger. The gray sting of spent gunpowder burned his nose. He sat with the mule for a long time, until the smell of burning rabbit meat and overcooked corn meal reminded him of his surroundings and the other realities of his time.

He rose up then on his bare feet and walked to the fire. He took the burned rabbit and bit into the charred, ashen flesh. It tasted black and dry, and it satisfied his hunger deliciously. He flipped the burnt corncake into the fire, and the orange and blue flame that erupted from its center delighted him. He took another bite of rabbit and turned his face toward the motionless mule. He thought for a moment about the absence of gold with which he would return to Agnes, but he did not worry about it, for now he knew what

54

he was capable of in the name of love, and Rev. Perser would know too, one way or another.

Benjamin Uriah and the Golden Gate Bridge

He was a tall man; some says as much as seven feet high. He weighed 28 English stones, meanin he was about as big as the mountain them stones come from. I knew him only a little, compared to Mr. Strauss. It was a quick thunder of fate what brought them two together, but it happened nonetheless.

Joseph Strauss had been goin about tellin folks he'd build 'em a bridge from Oakland clear to the peninsula of San Francisco. Most laughed. Some believed. And that's how Benjamin Uriah come into the picture.

San Francisco had come a ways towards big city from the time it were first named Yerba Buena. Maybe some of you didn't know of that first name. Means good herb. Yep, good herb. Stories have it that for most of its life the bay was so treacherous and the land so hostile that not much in the way of folks nor plants lived here, 'ceptin some big, plumb-shaped bulbs--good herb.

Well anywise, in 1847 it got a new name, San Francisco, named after the patron saint of animals, Saint Francis from Assisi. Sure 'nuff the very next year they discovered gold. You know, Sutter's Mill gold. Well, with gold, come the folks. In 1848, five hundred people lived in San Francisco. Two years later, that very same town lay claim to thirty-five thousand.

'Course, back then ships carryin every kind of skin colored man and lank necked beast found their way into that bay. That small mouth, accidentally named Golden Gate a hundred years before anyone thought to discover gold, was a monster. Millions of gallons a minute of freshwater dump transfers out to the saltwater sea. Them sailors called that mouth small, even though it is more than a mile across. Compared to the rest of the bay, I guess a mile ain't so great, but as you ponder puttin a bridge across a mile, high up enough for all them ships to pass under, and strong enough to stand up to the awful natural forces; well... But I'm gettin ahead from myself.

Almost since forever, people crossed the bay on the famous Kangaroo ferry; and that boat was somethin to see. Steam exhaled outta those two painted stacks, and that noisy, sloppy propeller churned slow as the tide, creatin a sound so comfortin, like a waterfalls, most folks didn't mind the 40 minute ride between San Francisco and Oakland. And boats remained the only way to cross the bay until 1936 when Strauss finally completed that wondrous bridge.

The first time anyone took notice to build a

suspension bridge was the decree made on August 18th, 1869, by Emperor Norton the First. Folks still says the old coot was queer in the forebrain, but he did prophesy the bridge. And no amount o' psychological schoolin can take that away.

The big war, around 1915, brung on the great war ships, and the bay got more and more congested. Mr. Jim Wilkins, one o' them strange Berkeley fellas, he writ a editorial in the San Francisco Bulletin callin out fer action ought to be taken on Emperor Norton's decree. Yep, he writes let's build a bridge to span the "Golden Gate."

In the next year, 1916, here comes Mr. Joseph Strauss hisself. Pompous, vain, rude engineer from Chicago, comes gallopin into San Francisco big as you please, and says, "I'm going to build your bridge."

He doesn't know, 'course, that San Francisco folks is all rebels, so ain't nobody can tell them a blasted thing, and certainly ain't nobody can tell them about their own bridge, even if it ain't built yet. Yessir, in the previous dozen years or so, this shameless San Francisco had rebuilt itself right on top of and in spite of the ashes and the rubble of that earthquake. That ain't the kind of city you walks into and start makin demands on.

But Strauss, he was short-tempered, and maybe that went with his bein so short, but that bully in him and that temper, well, fact is, it sorta endeared him. Mr. Joseph Baerman Strauss spent seventeen years, from 1916 to 1933, convincin and arguin to get hisself selected engineer for the bridge. Who wouldn't find endearment in that sort of persistence?

Still Waters

I first seen him in The Starfish. It were your typical low end dock bar, with most of us workin in some way with the boats, loadin, unloadin, anything we could get; it were the depression, you know. Inside was not too good lit, but nobody went there for the view. The bar spanned the whole length of the room, and most men drunk the dark, warm, steam-ale. We was honest folks, not prone to puttin on airs, so when Mr. Strauss began to make his appearances there, it didn't set well at first. He's a big talker. Says lots of words like he chews on 'em for a long time before he spits 'em out. And he don't really spit 'em out, more like he seduces 'em. You know, like they was special friends of his.

Fact is, we got used to him, and one night he was spittin out them fancy-dressed words, tryin to convince us that the city engineers was all wrong regardin the puddin stone in the bottom of the bay. That's when first I seen Benjamin Uriah. Far as I know, was the first time they met. It were a Saturday, I remember that, 'cause with no work on Sunday we was all sippin an extra mug or two. Maybe 'twas that which allowed us to tolerate Mr. Strauss's fancy talk, that and Jeannie Mae Loraedo, the most copious black-haired waitress on the docks. A fine white bubble of a moon made the bay all silvery and, truth be known, the smoke inside The Starfish sort of added to the special quality of the mood. I was standin about three men down-bar from Mr. Strauss, a distance safe enough from his extended words and close enough to listen in if I judged his topic interestin since whenever he got tired of bridge talk he'd take it upon hisself to

60

talk about other matters, all of which he lay claim to especial knowledge.

As I was sayin, me and Ted from over on Dock 12 was raisin our elbows to a foamy gulp when our view of Jeannie Mae bendin over a table was interrupted on account of the light from the door disappeared. Ted, he don't think so much about the loss of a little light and managed both to watch Jeannie Mae and finish his swallow. Me though, I turned away from the fanciful formulation of Jeannie Mae's waitressin posture and beheld a doorway stuffed solid with a ghastly big body what paused a moment to adjust to the darkness. He bent down to allow the small, blue hat on his head to pass under the door frame, and as he stood erect, I nearly choked on the excess of ale which spilled as I lifted my head another twelve degrees in order to catch the full view of his height.

There he stood, a bag in his hand, bigger 'en a bear rised up on hind legs smellin the wind. The darkness stunned him fer a moment, and he squeezed his eyes together like a crow about to strike. His big head turned, takin in the bar from one end to the other.

Jeannie Mae give that sweet squeak she sometimes made when somethin pleasured her, and she pulled herself away from old Harvey Grain so fast he darn near tipped out of the chair. She fluffed a bit of her hair back from her face, and blessed be the saints, in the process give us a view of her mamaries as profound as sunrise. She walked to him, not the least bit formal about his size, and asked what could she give him. By then, wasn't hardly a word in the place. Why between the spectacle of a giant stranger in our midst and the delicate display of Jeannie Mae's bountiful womanhood, wasn't really much left to talk about. The stranger smiled polite to Jeannie Mae, nodded his appreciation by tippin his finger against his cap, and then said clear as tap water, "I come to see Mr. Strauss, the Engineer."

Well, that done it. Every eye turned to the little mouse, Strauss, and fearin trouble, those what stood next to him, moved. It were obvious to even a stranger who Strauss was cause he was the only man in the place wearin a suit and tie. The stranger looked over the top of Jeannie Mae's head and peered at Strauss, and Strauss, courageous beyond most men, sipped his beer. Still, there wasn't much talkin, and the stranger, he walked over to Strauss and said to him, "I can help you build the bridge."

Over the years Strauss had heard all kinds of suggestions on how to build the bridge, but wasn't no record of anybody comin right out and sayin he could help. First of all, nobody really knew if a bridge could be built to span an entire mile, no common person leastways, and second, ain't no man in San Francisco careless enough to get Strauss goin on bridge talk lessin he had a good ear and a strong drink; so we wasn't sure whether to applaud the stranger or to rush him out of the place. But, before anybody gets any real idea towards action, Strauss says, "How do you plan to do that, sir?"

"I can prove there's bedrock under the puddin stone."

Well, sir, you coulda heard the footsteps of a

rat dancin on a tie rope it got so sudden and fiercely silent. Wasn't nobody in the city what didn't know that Strauss's most recent setback with the planners run around the topic of stability. Seemed like every expert 'cept Strauss believed the bottom of the bay was mud and silt, sorta like dark butterscotch puddin, with no rock for anchorin the piers. So the joke was you couldn't build nothin stable on puddin stone.

Well, Benjamin, he stood there with his sack, and Mr. Strauss, his eyes at just about the height of Benjamin's belly button, cranked his head back and lifted his chin upwards toward the ceilin and said to him, "Just what makes you think you can do that?"

Benjamin, he put his hand into the sack, and he pulled out this handful of a stone. In his hand it looked like a stone, but truth to tell, it probably weighed in at twenty-five pounds and was about the size of a June watermelon, all gray and hard lookin with jagged edges, like it been chipped and scarred with a pointed chisel.

Benjamin set the melon stone on the bar, and Mr. Strauss, his breath sort of stopped. Neither him nor Benjamin Uriah spoke. They just looked at that stone. In fact, we was all lookin at that stone, starin at it, a few men sippin at their draughts.

Since all of us was bein quiet, we just kept bein quiet, waitin for Mr. Strauss to tell us what's so special about that rock. He turned, real slow, looked up at Benjamin, and asked, "Is it from below?"

Benjamin nodded that big head of his, and he says matter of fact, "Yes."

Mr. Strauss says, more to himself than to

anyone in particular, "You know what this means?" He looked up at Benjamin's face, and he says, "Of course you know what this means. That's why you brought it to me." He looked again at the stone, touched it, and said to Benjamin, "Sir, you will have a job with me as long as you live."

Benjamin, he wrapped a big hand around Strauss's so that Mr. Strauss's hand disappeared inside it, fingers and all. But they shook hands vigorously, after which Engineer Strauss ordered a round of drinks for everybody in the house, which ingratiated us all the more to the little man. As he did so, he shouted out, "This granite confirms my belief that there is bedrock under the puddin stone. Gentlemen, we're going to build a bridge."

In about a week, he managed to call a meetin together of all the city fathers and the engineers. It was down to the city hall in San Francisco. Them fancy-pants types was dressed in their pressed, clean suits and soft ties and fresh-brushed hats. Ted and me walked into the gallery with Benjamin. We put our hats in our hands and sat down. Most folks was just talkin, waitin for the proceedins to begin, but you could feel some excitement in the buzz of the whispers and the plumes of smoke from the cigars. Me, I likes to smoke my pipe, so I smoked it.

We sat near the dividin wall which separated us from the officials, like the rail at church. It had dark oak spindles and a saddleback top rail about as pretty as the inside of an abalone shell. On the other side sat three tables, the corners pressed together to make the letter "U," one for Strauss on one side, one

64

for the other engineers on the other side, and one in the center facing all of us for the city council and the bankers. Strauss sat alone at his table with an ordinary brown box restin there, a little off to the side so's he could see.

Before too long, gets goin the meetin. Mr. Strauss, he explained how he had some new evidence regardin stability at the bottom of the bay, and then he sat down. The other engineers told how all their studies prove no pier can stand in the open ocean on unstable soil, and they talked for a good long time until I begin to think maybe all engineers likes to hear theyselves talk and not just Engineer Strauss. Truth be told, each one of them engineers was drove by one of two motives: either he didn't want the bridge a'tall, or he wanted to be the chief engineer hisself. Now, Mr. Strauss, he let 'em all talk, get their arguments down, and when they finally ended, they looked smug and restful. They all kinda turned their eyes toward Engineer Strauss, waitin, you know, for him to say somethin. But he don't do nothin. After about a minute of silence, the gatherin began to get a little twitchy, and some of them started to move their feet, nervous-like, so it sounded like the crunch of sand scrapin against the floor. But still, Mr. Strauss, he don't do nothin. He just sat there, smilin.

Finally, Professor Bailey Willis, that unhappy Engineer from Stanford, says, "Well, Mr. Strauss, are you going to speak to us, or not?"

Mr. Strauss, he kinda got up slow, did a small head-bow to the esteemed panel, ignorin the engineers at the other table, and opened the cardboard box. He pulled out the piece of granite what Benjamin Uriah give him, and you could tell by the size of the eyes of those engineers all openin up simultaneous that they knew what he had. And still, he don't say nothin; he just lifted that piece of rock and walked up to the middle of that center table, right in front of Supervisor Stanton, and he placed that rock, quiet and gentle, at the base of the microphone so it don't even make no noise. He paused a minute, and all them engineers was lookin at that rock with the same reverence Strauss and Benjamin give it at The Starfish. Then he turned to the left a little bit, to the secretary, and he said to him, "Mr. Secretary, you may draw up my contract. I will order borings in the morning."

Now most of you what's familiar with the history of the San Francisco Bay bridge knows what happened after that. The Pacific Bridge people, the Graham brothers, them Roeblin brothers from New Jersey, Moran and Proctor from New York, all manner of talented, hard-workin men come together to build a bridge unlike any other in the world. Once construction begun, it went on nearly 24 hours of every day, so you can imagine the atmosphere. Lots of people, public scrutiny, lawyers everywhere, and almost every part of the construction so new that we was as much inventin the thing as we was buildin it.

Benjamin made hisself valuable to Mr. Strauss, and to all of us as well. He never complained, and he took on dangerous work, especially if a man with a family was assigned to it. I suppose one sizable contribution Benjamin made concerned the trestle. In bridge buildin, the trestle is the roadway from the land out to the fender. The fender is a kind of skirt that goes in the water and around the pier to make a work area. If you can imagine cuttin both ends of a can off so's you got a can with holes at both ends, you got a picture of a fender. Imagine if you put that can in the middle of a mud puddle; you could take the water and mud out from inside the can while the rest of the mud and water lapped around it. That's how our fender worked; we put a big can in the ocean, and we pumped out the water and worked inside. That came later on, of course. First the problem with the trestle needed fixin. The first trestle was built sturdy, with big steel trusses. Problem was, them Pacific storms with the waves and the tides was so fearsome that those big trusses acted like flat boards tryin to hold back a spring river, and they crashed. This set-back caused some consternation among the engineers, and in the newspapers some speculation started to turn toward those what said it couldn't be done.

Late one night, a group of engineers, with Strauss in the middle of 'em, was drawin designs and hopin to find a solution. Benjamin, he knocked politely at the door, and Strauss jumped at him. "What is it, Benjamin? We're busy." Benjamin, he's used to Mr. Strauss's ways by now, so he ignored his temper. He walked past the sketches and the big coffee pot which never stopped boilin to Mr. Strauss's desk. He lowered one of them big hands and grabbed two of those round carpenter's pencils, yellow ones, which was restin in a glass jar. He laid the two pencils on the desk, and he grabbed Mr. Strauss's coffee cup right out from his hand. He balanced the cup across

67

both pencils, and it sat there, sturdy.

"Logs, Mr. Strauss," he said. "Use round logs to design the trusses. The water will spill around them, and the weight above will stay balanced." Of course, he was right as sugar, and by morning them engineers was prancin like roosters because they figured out a way to make the trestle work.

Benjamin's most important idea was also his most costly. In order to build the piers, the engineers designed the fender out of steel. Inside the fender the water held calm. But another problem arose when the engineers blasted the foundation stone to prepare the area for the fender. They shattered the rock and created fissures so that by the time they reclaimed bedrock, the fender had to rest at more'n 100 feet below mean tide, instead of the original depth of 65 feet. You might can imagine the meetins which that news generated. Especially come two big questions: how do you build a one hundred foot fender? and what do you do with the sixty-five foot one already built?

It were again at night, a lovely, star-lit May night, peaceful and cool, that Benjamin choose to interrupt Engineer Strauss. He come right to the point. "You don't need to design a new fender," he said. "Build sections of new walls made from concrete for the lower thirty-five feet. Rounded, with each section a little smaller than the one below it, like a teepee, and each section can be cemented in place permanently so that it can serve as anchoring points for the pier as well as a fender wall."

Strauss got the idea. The final concrete layer

was designed as a baseplate for the existing steel fender. Since they had to build under-water deadmen as anchoring points, the cost of those could transfer to the concrete walls, and Strauss turned a fiasco into another engineering wonder, for a lot less money than everyone at first thought. It went fine except for one thing.

Benjamin insisted on leadin the team of divers who set the panels. Even though each panel was small compared to the overall finished product, each section was about half the distance across a college football field. Under water, the divers moored themselves to anchors so as not to get carried off by the tides and river wash. Even then, they looked like round-headed, leathery kelp floatin sideways like a flag does. The first row of concrete sections went pretty good, and the men was gettin ready to set the second layer.

The divers come early, before sun-up. They checked gear, set weights, suited up. About sunrise, as a remarkable orange line of mornin spread across the horizon of water, the rest of the crews arrived. Tugboats blew inky clouds like bulls snortin black breaths from their circular nostrils. Sea gulls and pelicans flew about, but the noise of engines drowned their squawkin. The wind brought the smell of salt and fish and filled my lungs so's I thought I was breathin with gills. It were the finest day I could remember in months.

We dropped the divers straight into the middle of the fender. Once they reached bottom, we allowed 'em plenty of time to tie off and get ready.

Finally, the crane begun to lower the first

69

piece. Down below, Benjamin untied his lead and crossed over the top side of the wall. Now, of course, we speculate all manner of reasons for what he did, but at the time, nobody down there paid him no attention. What with everybody havin his own job to do anyway, and Benjamin bein who he was, people stopped questionin his ways months before. The fittin of the piece went so smooth nobody noticed that it killed Benjamin until the small cranes begun to pull the divers back to the surface. Benjamin was not at the end of his hose. Without nobody seein it, the section of wall set in place while Benjamin was still on the other side, his hoses and rope descendin from the center like everyone else's, looped over the wall, and when the new section dropped into place, it cut Benjamin's lines. He never did surface, and we never found the body.

Benjamin's loss shook engineer Strauss plumb to his shoes. Afterwards, he took it upon hisself to insure that nobody else died. Course, that ain't possible on such a big, wicked job. But he did invent lots of safety things with the same enthusiasm he designed that bridge, things like the safety net. Not only did he save about two hundred thousand dollars worth of equipment which might otherwise have sunk to the bottom of the bay, but that net saved another eighteen men's lives. Instead of droppin to their deaths in the deadly waters below, they climbed up the netting and went back to work. And maybe you heard about some of the other things: brought a decompression chamber to the hospital, doctors and nurses available on site, regular rest for the men;

Benjamin Uriah

things like that.

As time moved on, that bridge took on a life of its own. And everyone knows it's a beautiful son of a bitch, a wonder, a marvel of engineering, money, imagination, human sanity, and death. Ain't no great thing what don't charge for its greatness. In the history books they report that twelve men died buildin that bridge, but it ain't so. Thirteen died. Nobody talks about Mr. Benjamin Uriah. Bad luck. I believe I'm the onlyest one left holdin the secret, so I'm tellin it before my days is done. And there's another thing, too. In all the picture books they tell you that the reason the great Bridge is painted safety orange is so it stays in a state of good repair instead of it ever fallin into a state of disrepair. Now that's one reason for sure, just like Engineer Strauss said so. But there's some of us what believes there's another reason. Truth of the matter is, we believe that was his way to makin sure Benjamin Uriah could see it, no matter where he finally come to rest.

The Executor

This story is about Robbie Merton and his wife, Kathleen. It happened in the 60's, and nothing made the kind of sense you wanted it to back then. It was like things kept going wrong, and nobody was certain whether they'd ever go right again. But Robbie and Kathleen weren't like that at all. You could say they lived their lives in spite of circumstances, not because of them.

***

By the time we were seniors in high school, the Vietnam conflict had percolated itself into a sizable gathering, and Robbie and Kathleen got married. Robbie and I signed up on the buddy system, and we did basic and AIT together. Most everybody went in the service, except our friend Norval Smith. Norval was an okay guy, don't get me wrong, but with a name like Norval, we just knew he'd end up a lawyer. So nobody cared when he went to Penn State while we went to Fort Dix.

Robbie and I finished AIT, and as permanent duty, I went to Da Loc with the First Cavalry; Robbie went to Georgia with Kathleen. Robbie got this pansy job baby-sitting a bunch of ROTC cadets. About every 90 days, for six weeks, he'd help teach them how to be artillery captains. What did he do between camps? Hung out on the beach. He'd write me letters, and he always wrote, "Keep your ass down, GI," like it was our own personal joke or something. Loads of laughs, Robbie was.

I was base-camped near the DMZ in late March: monsoons, mosquitoes, salty food, and warm beer. Good grass, though, and plenty of it, but that didn't compete with Robbie and his stateside beach duty. I wrote him a letter saying gung-ho stuff like "Real men volunteer." I told him about this girl who took on the survivors of two platoons just after a firefight. She probably made enough money to feed her family for a year, but she couldn't walk, and her mama-san came with the old village buffalo to carry her home.

I feel bad about that letter now because Robbie never read it. He was in the hospital at Fort Sam Houston in Texas. Kathleen read it to him. That letter continues to embarrass me; the subject of prostitutes just didn't sit well with Kathleen.

I learned the details of Robbie's accident after I got home. Even now the irony of it seems peculiar.

As I said, it was near the end of March. Robbie had a new group of wimpy wonders at Fort Benning.

Robbie's Battalion CO, Lieutenant Colonel Mangino, was a typical lifer. The moment the lieutenant colonel found out there were VIP's on base, he ran to the commander and suggested a big show, allowing the new ROTC cadets to shoot some artillery rounds for the VIP's, two generals and a Congressman from Oklahoma. The base commander agreed.

It was set up for early evening because the smoke and the flash of the guns took on more of an ethereal hue in the twilight. No small detail went unattended by Lieutenant Colonel Mangino. It was a common exercise, and it should have gone without a hitch. Simple triangulation shot. Triangulation is how the gunners find a target. They know the location of the gun. That's one point. A point-man goes off a couple hundred meters to establish the second point. Then, using that old high school geometry stuff, they formulate some kind of scalene triangle and shoot the longest line to the third point, the target.

The evening settled in with the spring energy of dogwood blooms and magnolia blossoms. Robbie radioed his coordinates to the rookie ROTC's and waited for them to take a couple of shots at a tank 450 meters north and east. Unfortunately, the cadets were too new to be triangulating with a real Howitzer. Instead of coordinating the target tank, they targeted Robbie's bunker and lobbed a 108 right into the sand bags. The impact flung Robbie about the distance of four duce-and-a-half's laid bumper to bumper. It shattered most of his arteries and collapsed some veins, and it contributed a generous concussion which split the skull from just above his left eye to his ear.

Still Waters

He didn't win a medal, though. Even though it was war time, he was believed to be in a safe zone.

It was the reverberations and not the blast that did the damage, so Robbie's body was intact when they reached him. Internally, he was shattered, and, I will say this, when the doctors realized the extent of his problems, they signed off immediately and flew him to Fort Sam.

Fort Sam's a training hospital, so the Army wanted to perform some experiments on Robbie. New technologies, they said, and Kathleen gave them permission. They riveted a metal plate in his head where the skull had separated; they placed a small, nuclear-powered impulsor next to his heart to help it beat rhythmically; and they replaced the arteries around his heart with silicone tubing. To most everyone's amazement, he survived.

Of course, there were intermittent problems. His human parts only worked when the pump and the tubes worked, and occasionally they stopped; and without reason nor explanation they'd suddenly start again. Robbie became an interesting living experiment.

Kathleen went to Texas with him. She stayed by his bed six or seven hours every day, and read storybooks to him. After awhile, the nurses let her give Robbie his sponge baths. That's when they discovered his dick still worked.

***

It was not a surprise that Kathleen stayed by

Robbie during this entire incident. Their particular love arrangement formed when we were children. Kathleen was one of those rare red-haired girls with a child's face and a woman's eyes. There is no short way to explain Kathleen. Most of the thoughts I have about her don't have an anchor in time—she just always seemed a bit remarkable to me, and in a quiet sort of way, beautiful. Kathleen possessed Irish green eyes which she kept faithfully focused on Robbie. They were a pair, though, Kathleen as lithe and supple as a lynx, Robbie as short as a possum and just as tenacious.

When we were in seventh grade, Robbie and Norval and I stood in the shade under the maple tree in the corner of the school playground. The weather was pleasant, a bright sun and a few puffy clouds in a blue sky.

"I found a way to make sure I'm not late for school any more," Robbie said.

"Did you learn to fly over the trains?" Norval asked him.

We all laughed at this because Robbie lived on the eastern side of the railroad tracks. Sometimes he got stranded by the 7:20 train. That morning train took so long to pass through town that Robbie would be eighteen or twenty-two minutes late for school, depending on whether he walked or ran from the tracks.

Kathleen walked out of the sunshine to join us in the shade. A red cotton ribbon held her hair in a ponytail, and she carried a small brown bag with her lunch in it.

"How do you get by the trains?" Kathleen asked Robbie.

We were twelve years old; not quite old enough to figure out girls, and not quite young enough to keep on ignoring them.

Robbie looked at the three of us. Then he said to Kathleen, "I roll under them."

About that time the bell rang; time to stand in line for class. As we stood there, Norval said, "Prove it."

"At lunch," Robbie said.

Kathleen whispered loud enough for all of us to hear, "I'm coming." Sister Mary Gregory headed our way and there was no more time for discussion.

That's how it started.

Back then, you know, there weren't fences around schools, so taking off was easy. Of course not many people took off because eventually you had to face Sister Mary Gregory, and she held vastly more control over a child's behavior than a fence ever could. But we took off and said the hell with Sister Mary G-man, sounding to ourselves like we had just crossed the threshold of adolescence instead of the school property line.

We ran to the rail crossing at Center Street. Every day, at noon, the old Erie and Lackawanna rumbled through town at maybe seven or eight miles an hour, its cars full of shiny Pennsylvania coal for the glass factory. At the crossing, we watched the train coming from the south. Robbie ran across the tracks.

"Come over to this side," he called.

"Why?" Norval asked for all of us.

"We'll all roll under the train and get back to school before lunch is over."

Norval and Kathleen and I hesitated. The noon sun made the coal chips glisten, and the pounding of the steel wheels against the tracks began to get loud. The engineer pulled the air chain, and the steam whistle blew. Whooommm. . . Whooommm . . . A warning.

Kathleen moved first. She stepped over the rail, and I watched her feet along the tie, black with creosote and marred from random flying pieces of the granite bed. She jumped the rail on the other side with both feet at once and landed next to Robbie like a bull rider who jumps off and lands on his feet, knees bent. The train rushed closer. The whistle sounded again, and before it finished its warning, the long, high-pitched lunch whistle at the factory sounded. The pounding of the locomotive against the rails added rumbles to the whistles like fingers of hammers on a steel drum. Finally, from fear as much as from pride, Norval and I jumped across the rails just as the lunch whistle stopped and the locomotive rumbled by and the engineer hollered at us for being unsafe and he hung his head out the window with his elbow on the ledge and shouted "Stay back."

Robbie smiled. He was about the size of a schnauzer shorter than Norval and me, but he stood there like a leader. "Way to go," he said. I admit I felt pretty cocky, thinking maybe Superman couldn't have done what I just did.

The train's rhythm was insistent. Bump. . .bum-bum. Bump. . . bum-bum. Every time a set of wheels passed us, we watched the ties pop up and down a little, and the big spikes tightened and slacked one quick rattle at a time. Bump. . .bum-bum. Bump. . .bum-bum.

"Here's how it's done," Robbie said. "I get down close to the tracks. When the first wheel gets to my face, I count to three. It usually takes three counts for the back wheel to go by. I do that with two or three cars to make sure I've got the rhythm. When I'm sure I have it, I go with the next set of wheels. I count one. On two, I roll--off my shoulder around onto my stomach. Then I crawl over to the other rail. I do the same thing. Count. Get the rhythm, and roll out. By the way, when you're underneath, keep your ass down. Sometimes there are wires and pieces of chain hanging from the frame."

He looked at us. Our faces must have had that dense, mathematical look we got every time Sister Mary Gregory said division. He said, "Watch. I'll show you."

The rumble and pulse of the train persisted, and the noise of the wheels against the tracks resembled loud, rusty screeches. The backdraft between cars was mild, but gritty as sandpaper. Frankly, the whole idea scared the piss out of me.

Robbie knelt down and put his palms against an oily tie. He listened and counted.

One. . .two. . .three. . . The back wheels passed. He waited for the next set.

One. . .two. . . three. As the next set began, his legs tensed, and as the count of one left my head his body rolled under that enormous moving mountain, and he disappeared. We knelt down to peer between the wheels. He lay in the center, the tipends of his fingers pressed against a tie, his eyes squinted against the claustrophobic echo of the rolling steel. We watched him ease sideways. After the fifth car passed, he rolled out the other side, onto his stomach, onto the sidewalk. He lifted his head to watch us watching him.

Norval shook his head. "I don't believe it," he said.

Kathleen asked me, "Sal, are you next?"

I looked up at the passing cars, bouncing, rumbling, the white letters of Erie and Lackawanna gray from the coal dust. The train was a long one, longer than the 7:20.

"No," I said.

She didn't ask Norval. She just knelt down next to the track, like at confession. The wind from the passing cars caused her ponytail to jump a little. She bent forward onto her hands, and without waiting for three cars to pass, she caught the cadence of the next set of wheels and rolled under the train and when two more cars passed, she rolled to the other side with Robbie.

Robbie and Kathleen waved good-bye to Norval and me. They walked back to school. Norval and I waited for the train to pass, and then we walked to Sister Mary Gregory's office.

***

Robbie looked pretty good by the time he and

Kathleen returned home from Fort Sam. Of course, he had collected a few idiosyncrasies. First thing you noticed right away was his unusual speech pattern. He had developed a weakness for the s-sound. When he said Kathleen, he pronounced it Kassoleeen. He also developed a near insatiable craving for 7-UP. It was a clear substance, he argued, and therefore it answered the doctor's criteria for drinking clear liquids. When he requested a 7-UP, he arranged so many s's at the entrance that he sounded like a balloon letting the air out of itself; and his v's sounded like f's. So 7-UP sounded like ssssefen-up. Of course, he took a shocking number of colorful pills which Kathleen sorted by size and lined up on the left side of the fireplace mantle. Pills for thin blood, and pills to fool his body into accepting all the foreign materials inside him which kept him alive, and naturally pills to mend the side effects, and pills that quieted the side affects of those pills.

Robbie moved and talked real slow. It took him about fifteen minutes to work up to "Hello," and about an hour to wind up for a full fledged conversation. And it was like that for sex too.

Sex was about a three day affair at the hospital, two days for travel and preparations, and a third day for recovery. The doctors tolerated its engagement only once a month. They suggested once every two months, but that suggestion attracted little sympathy.

They scheduled it for weekends. On the first Friday of every month, Robbie and Kathleen drove north to the VA Hospital in Syracuse to have sex.

Friday evening, the nurses set two IV's in Robbie's arm; one dripped high potency vitamins to help him recover, while the other fed him a delicious mixture of drugs which calmed him and made him sleep. He slept all night and most of the Saturday morning in order to build up strength. At exactly two o'clock Kathleen and Robbie were left alone in the room. They had one hour. At exactly three o'clock, the doctor and nurses rushed into the room. They re-inserted the IV's. They monitored his heart, oxygen, blood pressure, blood flow, and, I suppose other pieces of information which were important to their experiments. They tested, watched, and charted Robbie back to a safe zone. Then he slept again.

Sometime between seven and eight at night, Robbie and Kathleen shared a meal. After that, they let Kathleen sleep with Robbie, but he was drugged and wired, so her snuggles and afterplay were limited to one-sided contact. On Sunday afternoon they drove home.

Now you might guess that this arrangement aroused slightly disparate sexual expectations than, say for instance, champagne and vanilla-scented candles. And you'd be right. Since it was either that or nothing, Robbie and Kathleen took it. They did alter the routine once when they decided to do something special for Kathleen's birthday. On that day, Kathleen crawled off the bed three and a half minutes early. She walked to the door. She smiled at Robbie, and opened the door. Then she ran, naked, into the hall swinging her arms up and down, letting her hands flap like a traffic cop with double-jointed wrists.

"Quick," she called.

The nurses and the doctor ran to her. They rushed her back into the room.

"What is it?" the doctor demanded.

Kathleen smiled. "We're finished," she told him.

The doctor raised his stethoscope and flicked the end so that the rubber flipped the tip toward the door. With that, a nurse placed a robe across Kathleen's back and escorted her out of the room.

***

It was going on toward two years since Robbie had exploded. I received a call from Norval Smith. He invited me to his office that Saturday morning. I arrived about 10:00. Norval and Robbie were waiting. Norval explained that Robbie had made a will, and he wanted me to be executor. It was an easy job, but an important one. I had to make sure the terms of the will were met. It was a simple will, they said. Robbie left everything to Kathleen.

"So why do you need me?" I asked.

"It's a formality," Norval explained. "But we're doing this exactly by the book. Robbie doesn't want to take any chances it might be contested."

Norval had checked with the state insurance commissioner and with the VA attorneys.

Robbie had received in the mail an invitation to buy life insurance. Naturally, since his accident, no insurance company that intended to remain profitable would touch him. The mail offer was a nice surprise. It turned out to be one of those occasional military-industrial SNAFU's. The Army sold its list of disabled vets to a Virginia insurance company with the stipulation that no one could be turned down for pre-existing conditions which were a result of military service. Of course, it was decreasing term coverage, and unfairly expensive. That was the strategy: for a lot of money a vet could buy a policy that from year to year was worth less and less. Eventually, most people figured this out and canceled -- exactly what the insurance company wanted. Norval said it was legitimate, and it fit into Robbie's plan. After the initial purchase, every six months a person could double his coverage, up to four hundred thousand dollars -- a hundred thousand maximum at first, two hundred thousand in six months, and four hundred thousand in a year. That's what Robbie did.

***

Robbie and Kathleen gave up sex that year. Robbie didn't want to take any chances.

Thirty days after the insurance company received the last premium, I helped Robbie get ready. Kathleen went shopping. I brought Chinese food, champagne, and three dozen red roses. I helped Robbie put on a new suit with matching vest, suspenders, a white shirt with French cuffs and cuff-links, and a cobalt blue tie with red dots all over it. Robbie insisted that these duties went with being executor, so I obliged. He even made me spit shine his old black shoes.

"Why are you wearing so many clothes?" I asked him.

He looked at me with that old twinkle in his eyes. He said, "I want Kassoleeen to take her time undreeesssssssing me." His head wobbled like one of those felt-covered doggies in the rear window of a car. He had grown uncomfortably weak and delicate, so it pleased me no end to see him joking.

When Kathleen's car pulled into the driveway, I stood up.

"You look terrific," I said.

"I feel great." He smiled at me. "Sssssssal," he said, "ssssstay happy."

I nodded and went out the back door.

Robbie and Kathleen made love for the last time. Naturally, I never discussed details with Kathleen, but I have speculated that they took as much time as they wanted, and that when they were finished they held each other for a long, long time.